This book belongs to:

....

....

Editor: Ruth Symons
Designer: Bianca Lucas
Managing Editor: Victoria Garrard
Design Manager: Anna Lubecka

Copyright © QEB Publishing, Inc. 2013

First published in the United States by
QEB Publishing, Inc.
3 Wrigley, Suite A
Irvine, CA 92618

A CIP record for this book is available from the Library of Congress.

ISBN 978 1 78171 134 7

Printed in China

The Not-So-Perfect Penguin

by Steve Smallman

Books
Are Fun

On a snowy, blowy island in the middle of the sea
lived a group of perfect penguins. They were
smart and **serious** and **sensible**.

All except for Percy, who was...

well...

not so perfect.

The other penguins ate their dinner sensibly.
But Percy always played with his food.

"Eat nicely, Percy!"
the biggest penguin said.

While the other penguins **waddled** along seriously, Percy **slid** on his tummy.

"Be careful, Percy," the oldest penguin grumbled.

The other penguins swam smoothly through the water, catching lots of fish. But Percy liked to jump and play, doing somersaults and landing with a big...

SPLASH!

"Look out, Percy," the smallest penguin said. "You silly penguin!"

When it was really cold, all the penguins huddled together.
Percy felt **warm** and **safe** in the middle of the group.

But then, **oh dear**, he needed to...

FAAAAAAAART!

"Ew, Percy," the penguins said.
"You smelly penguin!"

They went and stood away from Percy.

Percy waddled away sadly.
"My friends think I'm **silly** and **smelly**.
I'll never be **perfect** like them..."

The snow fell harder and the wind blew stronger.
"It's cold on my own," said Percy, shivering.

Percy made himself a new friend from snow and ice,
but the snow penguin wasn't very warm to cuddle with.

Without Percy, the penguins ate their dinner sensibly.

"It's so quiet!" the oldest penguin said.

They swam seriously, without splashing.

"It's rather dull!" the biggest penguin said.

They waddled along
in a straight line.

"It's a bit boring!"
the fluffiest penguin said.

"I wish Percy
were here," the
smallest penguin said.

"What will happen to Percy?" the oldest penguin said.
"He's all alone in the freezing cold." The penguins began to worry.

So they waddled off through the swirling snow to look for Percy.

In an icy cave, they found two snow penguins.
One had lost its beak, but the other looked familiar.

It was Percy!

All the penguins gathered around and cuddled him.
Slowly, slowly, the snow began to melt.

Drip... drip... drip.

When Percy's flippers were free of snow,
he stretched and then...
TICKLE...
TICKLE...
TICKLE!

The penguins all fell down laughing.

"Oh Percy," the smallest penguin giggled.
"It's good to have you back!"

Surrounded by happy penguins, Percy felt that
maybe he didn't need to be perfect after all.
His friends loved him just as he was.

NEXT STEPS

Show the children the cover again. Could they have guessed what the story is about just from looking at the cover?

Percy is playful, but some of his actions annoy the other penguins. Ask the children if they think Percy was annoying or if he was just having fun. Have the children ever annoyed somebody when they were playing?

Penguins live together in big groups called colonies. Many types of penguin live in the cold, icy regions of Antarctica. They huddle together to keep warm in the coldest winter months. Do the children think it was mean of the penguins to leave Percy out of the huddle? Have they ever ignored a friend who annoyed them?

Percy thinks he doesn't fit in because he's not perfect like the other penguins. Do the children ever feel like they don't fit in? Discuss what this feels like. Explain to the children that we're all slightly different but we're all good at something.

Were the other penguins happier after Percy left? Ask the children why they think the penguins decided to go and find him.

Ask the children which penguin is their favorite. Is it Percy? Or maybe it's the fluffiest penguin or the oldest penguin. How many times can they spot their favorite penguin?

All of the penguins are smart and sensible.
All except Percy, who is...well... not so perfect.

But when Percy leaves, things just aren't the
same without him. The penguins soon realize
there's more to life than being perfect.

Beautifully illustrated, Storytime introduces young
children to the pleasures of reading and sharing stories.
Discussion points for parents and teachers are also included.

RRP $12.95

ISBN 978-1-78171-134-7

9 781781 711347

A. H. Benjamin

Gill McLean

The Nearsighted Giraffe